this
little  ORCHARD
book belongs to

....

....

ORCHARD BOOKS
96 Leonard Street, London EC2A 4RH
Orchard Books Australia
14 Mars Road, Lane Cove, NSW 2066
1 86039 667 4 (hardback)
1 86039 744 1 (paperback)
First published in Great Britain in 1998
Copyright © Penny Dann 1998
The right of Penny Dann to be identified as the author and
illustrator of this work has been asserted by her in accordance
with the Copyright, Designs and Patents Act, 1988.
A CIP catalogue record for this book is available from the British Library.
Printed in Italy

The Wheels on the Bus

Penny Dann

little ORCHARD

The wheels on the bus go **round and round**

Round and round

Round and round

The wheels on the bus go
Round and round
All day long.

The people on the bus step **on and off**
On and off
On and off

The people on the bus step
On and off
All day long.

The driver on the bus says Move along, please!
Move along, please!
Move along, please!

The driver on the bus says
Move along, please!
All day long.

The riders on the bus go **bumpety-bump**
Bumpety-bump
Bumpety-bump

The riders on the bus go **bumpety-bump**
All day long.

bumpety-bump bumpety-bump

chatter chatter chatter

The children on the bus go **chatter chatter chatter**
Chatter chatter chatter
Chatter chatter chatter

The children on the bus go **chatter chatter chatter**
All day long.

The babies on the bus go
Wah! Wah! Wah!
Wah! Wah! Wah!
Wah! Wah! Wah!

The babies on the bus go
Wah! Wah! Wah!
All day long.

The parents on the bus go Sshh! Sshh! Sshh!
Sshh! Sshh! Sshh!
Sshh! Sshh! Sshh!

The parents on the bus go
Sshh! Sshh! Sshh!
All day long.

The wipers on the bus go
Swish swish swish
Swish swish swish
Swish swish swish

The wipers on the bus go
Swish swish swish
All day long.